Steven's Days of Adventures

iUniverse books may be ordered through booksellers or by contacting:

iUniverse
1663 Liberty Drive
Bloomington, IN 47403
www.iuniverse.com
1-800-Authors (1-800-288-4677)

Because of the dynamic nature of the Internet, any web addresses or links contained in this book may have changed since publication and may no longer be valid. The views expressed in this work are solely those of the author and do not necessarily reflect the views of the publisher, and the publisher hereby disclaims any responsibility for them.

Any people depicted in stock imagery provided by Getty Images are models, and such images are being used for illustrative purposes only.
Certain stock imagery © Getty Images.

ISBN: 978-1-5320-9573-3 (sc)
ISBN: 978-1-5320-9574-0 (e)

Library of Congress Control Number: 2020903475

Print information available on the last page.

iUniverse rev. date: 02/20/2020

Steven's Days of Adventures

ALFONZO MITCHELL III

ILLUSTRATED BY
IRIS MITCHELL & ALFONZO MITCHELL III

CHAPTER ONE

STEVEN GOES SWIMMING

YIKES!

Hi, I'm Steven! This is a story about how I overcame my fear of swimming........

When I was 7 years old, I was afraid of water. I didn't like it in my ears, eyes or nose.......
so guess what........I never swam. Swimming looked fun but I was just so terrified to put
my head under water. My mom and dad always took my sister and I to the pool and I
remember watching my sister have so much fun in the water but not ME.

One day, my mom asked, "Would you guys like to take swimming lessons?" Of course,
my answer was "NO." My mom didn't make me take lessons but my sister agreed
to the lessons. I went with my sister to her lessons and sat quietly on the side while
she learned to swim. It looked so fun but I was NOT putting my head in that water.
Every day, my sister would be so happy to get in that water and I just could not
understand why.

One day after my sister's lessons, I told my mom to stop by our community pool so I could try something. My mom gave me a strange look but I insisted. My mom stopped at the pool and I slowly walked into the gate. For a minute, I stood there and stared at the water and then I slowly stepped into the pool. There was total silence until my sister just ran up and jumped into the water.........SPLASH!

Finally, I just went for it. And guess what.........I swam from one side of the pool to the other side. It turns out that as I watched my sister during her lessons, I was mentally learning how to swim. It felt so good to overcome my fear of the water and I was beaming with pride.

After that day, my mom asked again, "Would you like to take swimming lessons?" I grudgingly agreed because I had not yet 100% overcome my fear of swimming. The next week, I began my lessons.

My swim teacher was tough and she kept saying, "Keep your head down......Keep your head down!" Then, once she saw that I could swim, she told me to go and jump into the 8 feet and swim to the other side. I ALMOST LOST IT! Again, I was terrified and my worst fears had come true, I.....WAS......GONNA........DROWN!

My teacher wasn't gonna let me off easy so I had to do it. I was waiting for my mom and dad to step in and save me but they were quiet. I slowly walked to the 8 feet side of the pool. I started talking to myself and I kept saying, "You can do this Steven....... You can do this Steven......You can do this Steven!"

Finally, I just jumped.............

Time stopped and I thought I was already dead. When I realized I couldn't touch the bottom of the pool, I panicked. I began flapping and screaming and even grabbed onto the side of the pool cover. I could hear my teacher screaming, "Stop, you're gonna break it, you're gonna break it!" But I didn't care, I was just trying to survive.

Once I realized no one was gonna save me and that I was all alone in the middle of the ocean, my instincts kicked in and I swam as fast as I could to the other side of that pool. Although I was slightly embarrassed, I was once again proud of myself for overcoming my fear. Well........maybe not quite overcoming my fear but instead saving my own life.

I looked over at my parents and they were both beaming with smiles and giving me thumbs up. I MADE IT......I SURVIVED!

GET OFF STEVEN!

I didn't want to go back to lessons the next day but my parents made me. I thought they were trying to torture me. Couldn't they see that I needed to quit these lessons? Didn't they see me almost drown yesterday? Didn't they know that I was NOT jumping into that 8 feet again?

Obviously NOT............

I finished my lessons that week and jumped into the 8 feet at least 5 more times and I survived all 5 jumps.

Now that I am almost 9 years old, I am a great swimmer. It's still not my favorite thing to do and I still don't like water in my eyes, ears, and nose but I can swim and I am no longer afraid of the water. When my friends come over to swim, I jump in and have fun with them and I am able to save myself from drowning.

So, "IF I CAN DO IT, YOU CAN TOO............"

CHAPTER TWO

STEVEN GETS A PET

Hi, this is a story about me and my first Pet.......

When I was younger, I always wanted a Pet. My sisters and I begged and begged my parents for a Puppy. Our parents didn't think we were responsible enough for a Puppy. "Why would they think that?" It's not like we leave our stuff all over the house OR we have to be told when to take a shower OR we don't cook our own food. Hmmmm...... well maybe I understand their point just a little.

My mom asked, "Can we start with a fish?"........... "No Way, I said, "Fish are boring." She asked, "How about a Lizard?"........"Nah but maybe a Snake," I said. I could tell by the look on her face that a Snake was out of the question.

Mom kept suggesting everything except a Puppy and none of them were making us happy. She was trying to wiggle her way out of a Pet but we had other plans.

One day, mom came home with a BIG surprise! There was a cage, some food and a Pet. It was a Hamster and we immediately named him Hamsty!

He was the cutest animal we had ever seen. He had short furry, tan hair and the brightest eyes ever. It wasn't a Puppy but we were Super Duper Happy. Mom even bought a little round exercise ball so he could run around the house in it. He ran and ran and ran..........

2 days after we got Hamsty, my cousins came over and my mom specifically said, "Do not take that Hamster out of the cage." Before mom could get down the stairs, guess what.........my cousin had Hamsty in hands. We screamed because mom had us terrified of what would happen if Hamsty got loose in the house. Dad ran upstairs and put Hamsty back in the cage so our crisis was averted.

3 days after we had Hamsty, I woke up in the middle of the night and I kept coughing. My nose felt like it was all closed up and I couldn't catch my breath. Mom came in my room to check on me and she looked pretty scared. Mom had to get the breathing machine and give me allergy medicine. She also took me to the Emergency Room just to make sure I was okay.

Well, you know what happened next, right? As mom said it, "HAMSTY HAD TO GO!" Turns out I was allergic to Hamsty or maybe I was allergic to his bedding but whatever it was, Mom wasn't taking a chance. My sisters and I were so sad but Mom said, "If I have to choose between Steven and a Hamster, I choose Steven!" Oh Well, you can't argue with that.

Mom packed up all of Hamsty's stuff.........his cage, his food, his bedding, his exercise ball, and of course Hamsty. She took him back to the store and we never saw him again.

It was a Sad, Sad Day for our Family!

We still have pictures of Hamsty and we think about him often. Since he left, we have asked Mom for more pets but she keeps saying not yet. I think she's scared but don't tell her I told you.

I really want a Puppy or maybe even that Snake but even if it never happens, I still have my Family and that makes me Happy.

Maybe one day I will get a pet or even after I grow up, I can get one for my kids. Hopefully, they won't be allergic but if they are, "THE PET HAS TO GO!" Besides, Fish aren't so bad, right?

In the end, I had to learn to be Flexible because Mom said, "You can't break something that Bends!"

Oh Well, I guess we will get a Fish!

So, "IF I CAN DO IT, YOU CAN TOO............"

CHAPTER THREE

STEVEN PLAYS SOCCER

Its' me, Steven again and this is a story about my first time playing Soccer..........

When I was in Kindergarten, my parents took me to Taekwondo class where I learned to chop, kick, and scream. I liked it but I eventually got bored. Mom said I could transfer my classes to my sister so we did. On the first day that we took my sister to class, she said, "I'm sleepy today, lets come back tomorrow." Well, that was the last day that we went to the Taekwondo School. Mom said, we were wasting her time.

When I was in first grade, Mom and Dad signed me up for Basketball at the church in our neighborhood. It was fun and my Dad even coached. I was fast, really fast...... But I'm not bragging. Mom said the games were funny and I asked her why but she wouldn't tell me. Now that I am older, I think she was laughing because our team wasn't good.

After Basketball was over, I asked Mom if I could try Soccer. She gave me a strange look and asked, "Why?" I didn't have a good answer, I just wanted to try it. Mom said Okay and she signed me up for the next Soccer season.

On my first day of Practice, I was fast, really fast.......but I'm not bragging. My coach asked if I had played before but I had never played Soccer. Once the games started, I was super excited. I was so good that my team won all of our games and I think it's because I was fast, really fast........ But I'm not bragging.

Before every game, I would get nervous, really nervous. My stomach felt funny and my chest would get tight. Mom said I had butterflies in my stomach but that didn't make sense because butterflies would die in there, right? Well, it happened before every game, every time. I would try to calm my nerves but nothing worked. I finally noticed that my nerves calmed down usually about half way through the first quarter of the game after I did some running. So I started warming up and running around before every game and it worked. I still got nervous but the warm ups helped.

Butter-
flies

Everyone kept wondering if I had played Soccer before, even my parents were shocked at how good I was. I couldn't explain it, I just knew I would be good. My feet felt just like my hands out on that Soccer field and I was loving every minute of it.

Of course, my parents signed me up for the next season and the next season and every soccer camp they could find. They said that I had a Natural Talent and that we needed to nurture it. I thought, "Here we go again with these big words that I don't understand." I didn't really care what "nurture" meant, I just wanted to play Soccer.

One day, we lost a game and I cried. I couldn't control myself and I had never felt anything like it. I couldn't catch my breath either. Mom said I was super passionate about the game and that I needed to work through my emotions and try to control it. "What?" All I knew was that these feelings were coming out of nowhere and I couldn't control a thing. My teammates would look at me like I had three heads and not even the embarrassment could stop me from crying.

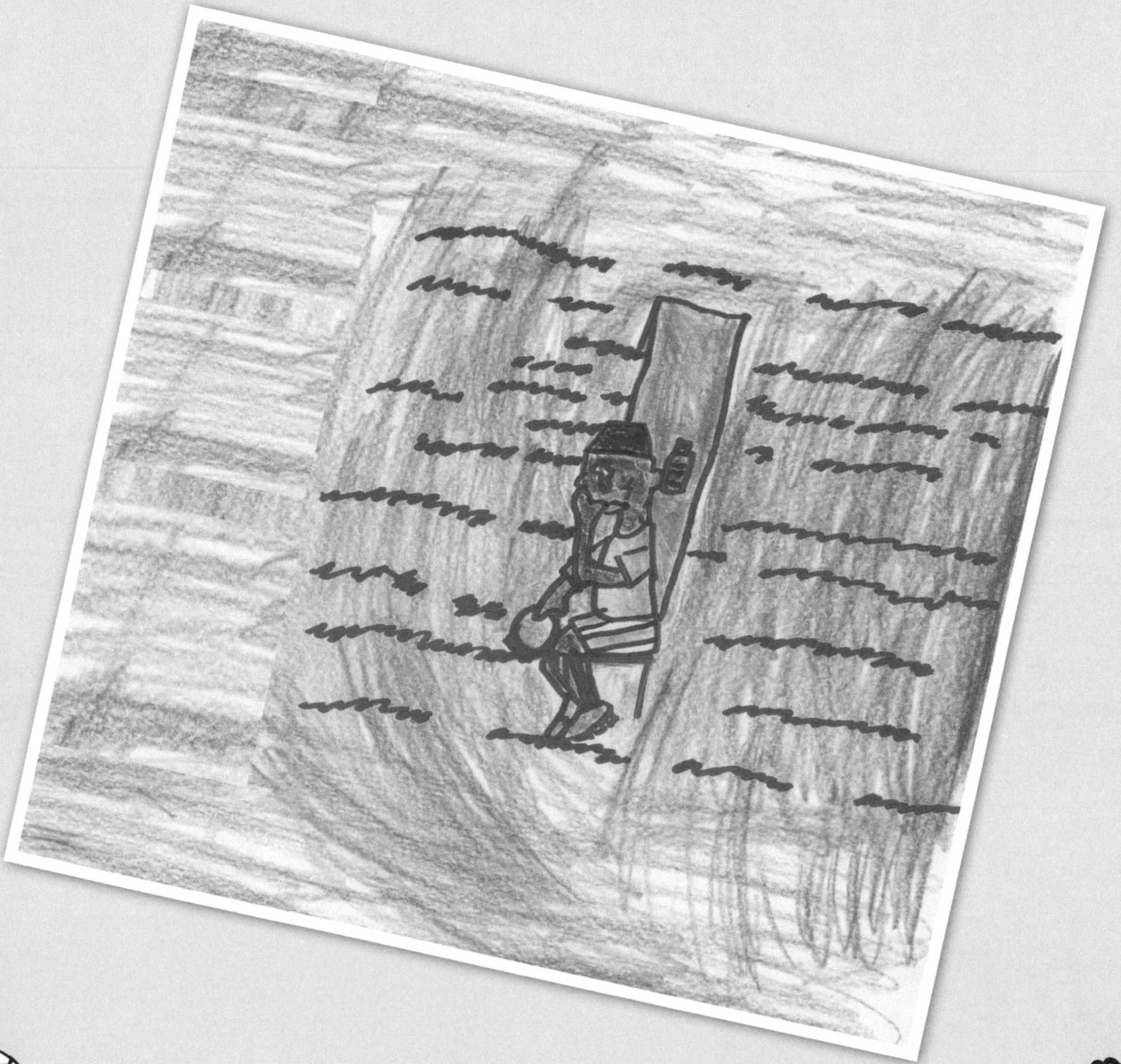

The crying happened a few times.......when I lost a game, when I missed a shot, when the other team scored.......the pain was excruciating and I couldn't do a thing about it, I thought.

One day, Mom said, "Steven, you must work on your emotions. We cannot elevate you to another, more competitive league until you are mature enough to handle it." BIG WORDS! Her face was serious so I knew this was important stuff that she was telling me. She told me to pay attention and come up with strategies for coping with my emotions. I had to give her two strategies that I would try for the next game. Soccer was turning into school work so I really thought about quitting but I knew my parents wouldn't allow it.

As I played more and more games, I did pay attention and I did come up with strategies and I did get better. One strategy was to look over at Mom and Dad when I felt myself getting anxious. We came up with a secret hand symbol that seemed to calm me down. I even started talking to myself, in my head of course, when I felt the anxiety building. I would tell myself, "It's just a game Steven, just have fun."

Well after much practice, I can say that I am much better at controlling my "breakdowns," as Dad called them. Mom and Dad even moved me to a more competitive league and I still love Soccer. I am still fast, really fast and I am truly a Good Soccer Player and I am bragging just a little. I am proud of myself for working through my issues and overcoming my emotions.

So, "IF I CAN DO IT, YOU CAN TOO............"

36

Printed in the United States
By Bookmasters